Atheneum Books for Young Readers
An imprint of Simon & Schuster
Children's Publishing Division
1230 Avenue of the Americas, New York,
New York 10020
Text copyright © 2004 by James Carville
Illustrations copyright © 2004 by
David Catrow
Book design by Ann Bobco
The text for this book is set in Meta.
The illustrations for this book are
rendered in watercolor and pencil.
Manufactured in the United States of
America
First Edition
10 9 8 7 6 5 4 3 2 1
Library of Congress Cataloging-in-
Publication Data
Carville, James.
Lu and the swamp ghost / James Carville
with Patricia C. McKissack ; illustrated
by David Catrow.— 1st ed.
p. cm.
"An Anne Schwartz Book."
Summary: During the Depression in the
Louisiana bayou, a curious young girl
helps the "Swamp Ghost" that her
cousins warned her about and finds
herself with one good friend.
ISBN 0-689-86560-0
[1. Friendship—Fiction. 2. Tramps—
Fiction. 3. Depressions—1929—Fiction.
4. Louisiana—History—20th century—
Fiction.] I. McKissack, Pat, 1944–
II. Catrow, David, ill. III. Title.
PZ7.C2627Lu 2004
[Fic]—dc22
2003014679

To my wife, Mary Matalin, who has given me
my life's two great gifts, her love and our children
— J. C.

To Mark Fredrick McKissack— WELCOME
— P. C. M.

For Deborah; happily we go, hand in hand
— D. C.

A NOTE ABOUT THE STORY

My mama's real name was Lucille, but everyone called her Miz Nippy. In this story you'll come to know her simply as Lu. She grew up in rural Louisiana during the Great Depression, and even when she was a little girl, she was strong and adventuresome. She wasn't afraid to go exploring or to make new friends or to help those who were less fortunate. As an adult she went door-to-door selling encyclopedias, even in the part of town where black folks lived. For a white woman in Louisiana in the 1950s, this was rare behavior. The money she made helped put me and my seven brothers and sisters through school.

When I was a little boy, my favorite stories were the ones Mama told about the adventures she had growing up. After supper she'd go sit in her rocker on the porch and call to us to gather round, using the French word she'd heard from her mama. *"Approche!"* We'd come sit by her feet and wait for the stories to begin. Now that I have two little girls of my own, I want to share one of my mama's stories with them, and with you. And so, *approche . . .*

—James Carville
Washington, D.C.

james carville

Lu and the Swamp Ghost

with
patricia c. mckissack

illustrated by
david catrow

AN ANNE SCHWARTZ BOOK ◦ Atheneum Books for Young Readers ◦ NEW YORK • LONDON • TORONTO ◦ SYDNEY

Mama named her Lucille Ray-Jean, after her two *grand-mères*. Papa said that was way too much name for such a tiny baby, so he took to calling her Lu. She'd been as curious as a Louisiana judge since the moment she could talk.

"Mama," Lu asked one morning while helping hang out the clothes. "Are we poor?"

Mama had a ready answer. "You're never poor if you have a loving family and one good friend."

Lu had lots of family, but not one good friend. *Maybe I'm just a little poor,* she figured.

"Why do you ask?" Mama wanted to know.

"I heard people talking about the Depression at the general store. What is a Depression, anyway?" Lu asked.

"Hard times," Mama said, shaking her head. "People out of work, no jobs."

Lu thought about that. Everybody in her family worked. Mama and Grand-mère were always busy in the house or garden. Sister milked the cows, and Lu gathered eggs from underneath the setting hens. Papa grew vegetables and sold them at the market. Even Binky, their hound dog, had a job announcing all strangers.

Deciding that the Depression was nothing for her to worry about, she skipped off to help Papa check his turkey traps.

TUR
NIP

The cypress woods were always full of wonderful sounds and smells. All around things fluttered, creeped, and slithered.

Lu skipped up beside Papa, and her movement scared a fat frog from one lily pad to another. Just then, a water snake raised its head, but the frog sprang away. "Now, ol' Mr. No Hips, you'll have to find something else for supper!" she shouted, clapping her hands. "Papa, how come snakes eat frogs?"

"All living things have to eat to stay alive," he explained. "Snakes eat frogs, frogs eat bugs—"

"And bugs eat US!" Lu laughed as she swatted at a mosquito.

Farther into the swamp Lu noticed something else. "Papa, how come the leaves of the sycamore tree are turning inside out?"

Papa wiped his brow. "Means it'll rain 'fore noon."

There wasn't a cloud in the sky.

As Papa worked, Lu walked ahead. Suddenly the air felt thicker. The sky grew darker. A worrisome mosquito buzzed in her ear. Otherwise it was quiet—too quiet.

Lu was about to turn back, when suddenly someone . . . or something . . . rose up in front of her. The thing was covered in mud from head to toe. Leaves, twigs, and feathers stuck to it. And it smelled awful, *phew-whee!*

Lu's cousins had told her about a creature called a swamp ghost, who gobbled up nosy little girls who strayed too far from home. She'd never believed them before, but now here was one standing right in front of her—a genuine, for-real swamp ghost.

"Please don't take me away, Swamp Ghost," Lu pleaded. She shut her eyes and waited for the worst.

At last came the answer. "Why shouldn't I?"

Lu thought hard. "Because I'm way too skinny to have much flavor. You need a good pork chop."

"You got pork chops?" said the ghost.

Lu opened one eye and then the other. "I can get you some."

"Then do it," he demanded. "And you'd better come back, and don't tell a soul, or I'll come after you." With that, the swamp ghost melted into the bushes.

Papa was right, after all. It stormed. Lu was from foot-to-foot till it was over.

Soon as she could, she filled a basket with lunch leftovers, slipped out the back door, and followed the path to where she'd last seen the dreaded creature. Shaking a little, she called, "Swamp Ghost, I'm here!"

The ghost appeared from out of the shadows. He snatched the basket without a thought of saying thank you. Lu watched him shovel red beans, rice, and corn bread into his mouth faster than a hog slurps down slop.

Lu couldn't resist asking just one little question. "Papa says all living things have to eat to stay alive. But you're *dead,* so how come you need to eat?"

The ghost studied her, his eyes the color of a summer sky. "Maybe it's 'cause we think we're still living, so we get hungry like the people we used to be."

That made sense to Lu. Still, there was something different about this ghost. He wasn't nearly as big and scary as a ghost should be. Moving in for a closer look, Lu snapped her fingers. "I got it! You're a kid ghost, aren't you?"

The creature pulled himself up tall. "I'm still big enough to swallow you whole and spit out the bones. Bring more food tomorrow or that's what I'm gonna do!" And he disappeared into the woods.

The next day Lu did her chores early, then packed crab cakes, biscuits, and a piece of Grand-mère's apple pie, and set out for the woods.

"Yoo-hoo, Swamp Ghost!" she called, and he appeared, looking tired and even dirtier than before.

"Thank you for coming," he said softly.

"Why, that's mighty fine of you to say," said Lu. "You're welcome." Then she added, "My name is Lu. What's yours?"

"Just keep on calling me Swamp Ghost."

"Do you have a family, Swamp Ghost?" Lu asked.

He licked his fingers. "Nope. Just me."

"Do you have one good friend?" Lu went on, remembering Mama's words.

"Nope again."

Nobody should be that poor, Lu thought sadly. *Not even an ugly swamp ghost.* "I've got a great big family, but I don't have a friend either," she told him.

They walked along the bayou, watching an alligator watching them, and a white heron perched on a cypress knee. Lu tried to see how long she could stand on one leg like the heron. The swamp ghost tried too. She fell. He fell. Their laughter echoed through the lowlands and startled a flock of swallows.

"No disrespect," Lu said, "but you're not a very good ghost. You got no chain to rattle. You don't go *Ooooooo*. You even laugh and play."

"I look scary," said the ghost, sounding defensive. "Scared *you,* didn't I?"

Lu fanned him away. "I aine a-scared of you one bit. That's the problem. . . . But let me noodle on how we can fix it." And she skipped off, leaving the swamp ghost by the side of the path.

Early next morning family members began arriving at Lu's house—all come to mend Papa's barn roof. Lu had to help, but that didn't stop her from thinking about the swamp ghost. On toward afternoon she hit upon what to do.

A big table was spread out on the screened-in porch. *"Approche!"* hollered Grand-mère. That one word meant, "Come to the table. Time to eat!"

Gathering hands, Papa said grace, then put in, "As my mama taught me, though times be hard, a person is rich when he has a loving family and one good friend."

My poor swamp ghost! Lu thought. *He may have no family, but he does have a friend.* Quietly she eased away from the table, loaded a basket, and lifted a key from a hook on the wall.

Lu rushed through the deep, dark woods. In her haste she never noticed that the sycamore leaves had turned inside out.

"Oh, Swamp Ghost! It's me!" she called. From behind a cypress he appeared. He ate while Lu shared her plan. "I've found a place where you can hide out and learn to ghost proper-like. Papa owns a houseboat on the backwater slue."

The swamp ghost followed Lu all the way to the houseboat. Inside it was musty, but there were two nice-sized rooms and a good roof. "You can practice your moaning and groaning right here," Lu said, adding, "Who knows, if you get good enough, one day you might even haunt a castle."

Thunder rumbled. "Uh-oh! I got to go," she said. "The swamp is no place to be in a storm."

"Thank you, Lu. You've been kind," said the swamp ghost. He held out his hand for the girl to shake—and she slapped a bar of Mama's lye soap in it.

"Use it," she said, laughing, and bounded off.

The storm closed in fast. Midway home the heavens opened. The driving rain made it impossible to see, and the ground beneath Lu's feet became liquid. Poor Lu lost her footing and fell. Mud covered her and filled her nostrils. She tried to breathe, she tried to get up, she tried to find something to grab on to. She tried not to sink . . . down . . . down . . . down.

Suddenly a hand grabbed her arm. It tugged at her, lifting Lu upright. *Pull. Pull.* Was it Papa? Lightning flashed, and she could see a figure that looked like a boy. There wasn't time to ask all the questions that filled her head.

Lu dragged herself after him, back to the houseboat.

Safe inside, she sunk onto a stool and caught her breath. "I'm grateful for your help," she stammered. And then Lu asked the question that had been hovering inside her for days. "I got to know. Are you a swamp ghost or not?"

A smile flickered across the boy's face. "What do you think?"

"What happened to all the ugly that was on you?" she wanted to know.

"I smeared myself with mud to keep mosquitoes from eating me alive in the swamp. The rain washed it off."

Lu listened carefully, looking into the familiar bright blue eyes.

The boy continued. "My name is Philippe, and I'm really from Baton Rouge. No folks. Been riding the rails looking for work. Found my way here." He hung his head. "This Depression has been mighty hard on me. And I'm truly sorry you almost got hurt."

While they talked, the rain stopped. In the distance Lu could hear Papa calling her name.

"I'd better go," Philippe said, heading out the door. "Thanks for being such a good friend."

Long about now Lu was feeling mighty rich. "Wait," she said. "Why don't you tell Papa your story? He can always use a hand in exchange for room and board."

She paused a moment, then giggled. "And don't worry, your secret is safe with me. Papa need never know you're a swamp ghost trying to pass yourself off as a boy."

And with that she grabbed Philippe's hand and
rushed to introduce her family to her good friend.